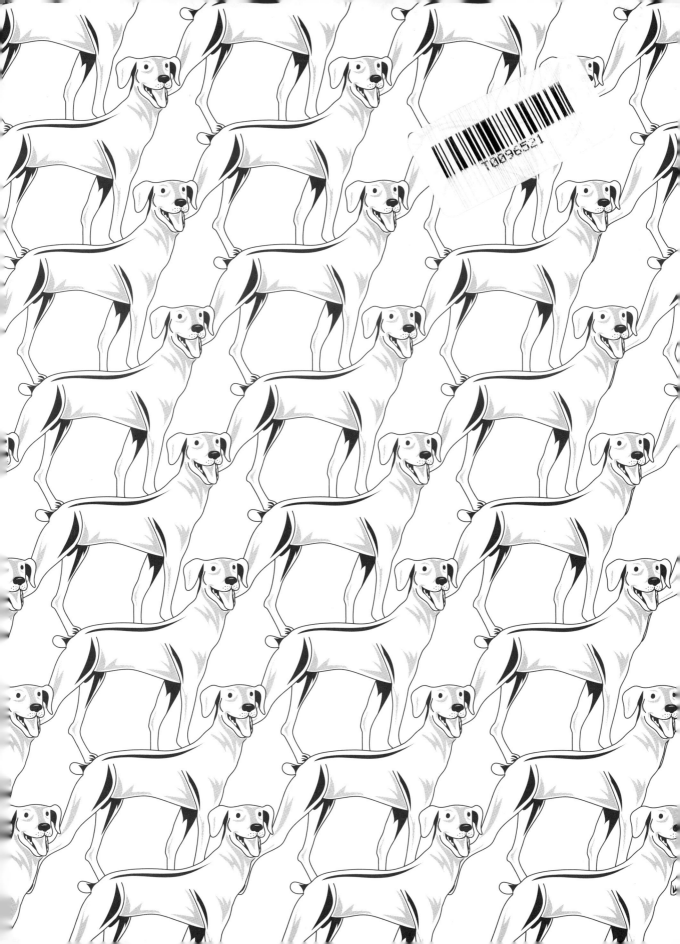

HOW TO TRAIN YOUR HOOMAN

A DOGGIE HANDBOOK

by Leia

mc Marshall Cavendish
Editions

"Man really is a dog's best friend. Especially when Man has a pocket full of treats."

Maggie Mayhem

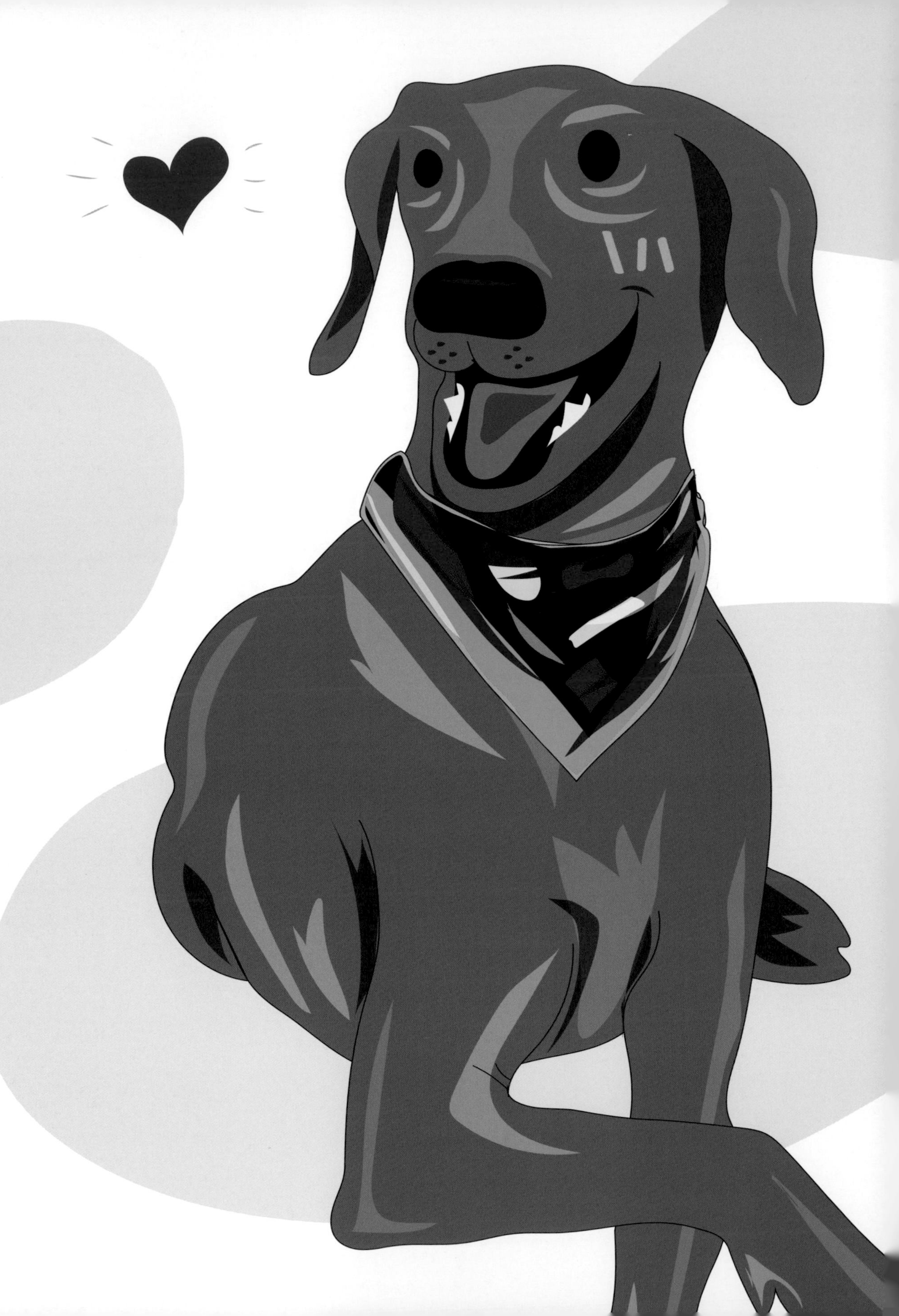

Hi everyone!

My name is Leia and I am a rescue dog.

Ever since I adopted my hooman,
I have picked up a lot of very useful
and effective training tips to help
him adapt to our world.

Training is most important if you want
to live harmoniously with your hooman.

I hope, through this handbook, that you'll
be able to get the most out of your own
relationship with your pawrents.

xoxo

Choosing the right hooman is very important.

6

Are you an active dog that needs plenty of exercise?

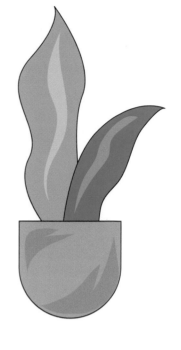

A lap dog that prefers cuddling and snuggling?

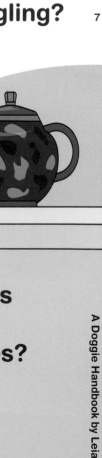

Or one that loves hanging out at hipster dog cafes?

A Doggie Handbook by Leia

If you're the sociable type,
then you should pick a FAMILY.
The more hoomans in the house,
the more hugs and cuddles.

8

love

I prefer not to share my hooman so I picked one who lives alone.

9

If you don't mind mini-hoomans crawling around you, a family with kids (sometimes called 'children') might be suitable.

(Note: some kids can be rather loud and noisy)

A Doggie Handbook by Leia

Make training fun for your hooman.

**If they enjoy their training,
they will be more willing to learn.**

10

**Hoomans respond well to
positive reinforcement so we
should always encourage and
reward their good behaviour.**

For example, I went to the front door and whined, so my hooman got up from his chair and opened the door for me.

11

Correct response!
I rewarded him by doing potty in the garden, doing the zoomies and giving him a big wet lick, which made him very happy!

A Doggie Handbook by Leia

Hoomans communicate with a variety of sounds called 'words'.

These are some of the more important ones:

EAT ... TREAT ... BONE ... DINNER ...
all mean the same thing – FOOD

WALK - we are leaving the house!

STAY - don't move. This could sometimes be followed by a 'SIT'. Hoomans will sometimes ask you to do random things like this.

Just make them happy and oblige them. You might get a treat for your effort!

12

13

COME - this usually follows a 'STAY'.
It means your hooman wants you to go to them.
Again, do it to make them happy. More treats!

NO - hoomans use this word very often.
I think it means they approve!

For example, if you are chewing on their favourite shoes and they say 'NO', show enthusiasm by wagging your tail excitedly and continuing with more gusto. This will cause them to raise their voices in excitement.

Always aim to please your hooman!

A Doggie Handbook by Leia

Communication is very important because you need to be able to let your hooman know what you want.

14

Sometimes, you don't need verbal communication to get your point across.

All you have to do is stare at your hooman, tilt your head and open your eyes wide. This usually makes them happy.

For example:
When your hooman is having dinner, sit in a corner and stare at him with your saddest look. He might get up and give you a doggie treat.

Reward him with a big smile and vigorous tail wag.

Hoomans learn best when they are rewarded for their efforts.

Is your hooman always going out without you?
If you suspect that they are planning to leave
the house, stare at them with big soulful eyes
to make them perform a sit/stay.

*(Pro Tip: If your hooman does not return eye contact,
walk in front of them and rub your body against their leg.
You can try sitting on their foot too.)*

17

18

'If I can reach it, I can eat it.'

Train your hooman to keep all their own personal things (like flip flops and shoes, smelly socks and gym sneakers, books and homework ... and hooman food*) out of our reach.

*Some hooman food can be very harmful to us dogs. We should train our hoomans to keep them away from us. These include items like chocolate, grapes and raisins, onions and nuts.

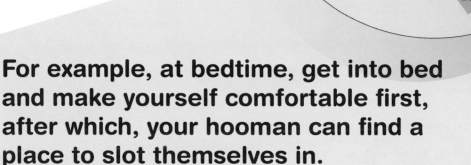

*'What's mine is mine.
What's yours is mine too!'*

**If you adopt a hooman, you
must teach them to share.**

20

**For example, at bedtime, get into bed
and make yourself comfortable first,
after which, your hooman can find a
place to slot themselves in.**

**Once they have learnt this, you can
apply it to any furniture in the room.**

**I make my hooman happy by waking
him early in the morning, so that he
is never late for work. You can do this
by licking their face. They love this.
You can also try sitting on them.**

Note: Even if you are in deep sleep, always wake when you hear the fridge opening.

A Doggie Handbook by Leia

It is important for dogs to keep their hoomans fit and healthy. We do this by taking them on regular walks.

Walks expose us to new experiences and new people.

I love my daily walks because I can sniff around for the latest gossip, chase the odd squirrel (or cat, or mouse) and bond with my hooman.

You should always keep your hooman on a lead, to keep them safe. That way, they do not wander off and get lost, or worse, get hit by a car!

You can play 'fetch' with your hooman.
All you need is a tennis ball.

Encourage your hooman to throw the ball
for you to chase by dropping it at their feet.
Keep repeating.

Ball games are great for improving your
hooman's strength and stamina.

All hoomans love a good game of tug of war. Bring your favourite toy to them, but don't allow them to pull it away from you.

This is a great way to help them burn off excess energy.

My friends have a great 'hide-and-seek' game they play with their hoomans who are a little unfit.

Wait for the moment when your hooman is distracted (looking at their mobile phone or talking to their friends) and has carelessly dropped your lead, then take off quickly and run and hide. You don't want to run too far, though, in case you get lost.

I guarantee your hooman will run faster than you have ever seen. You know they love this game because they will flap their arms about and shout loudly in excitement till their faces turn bright red.

A Doggie Handbook by Leia

28

Belly rubs are also a great form of exercise for your hooman.

Repeated belly rubs every day will help with their coordination.

You can also keep your hooman fit by making them open and close the doors a few hundred times a day

Stop suddenly when your hooman is walking behind you, especially if they are carrying something. This is a good test of their reflexes.

Hoomans rely on us doggies to protect them, so we need to always be on the lookout for suspicious characters (like the postman, the delivery man, the plumber or the cat from the next street).

Keep them away with a stern warning bark (or three).

You must also check all incoming bags (even those carried by your hooman) for anything suspicious.

Escort your hooman everywhere, even to the toilet, just in case they get lost.

Hoomans have a very strange ritual called 'baths'*.

If you are unfortunate enough to be forced into one, you can neutralize the strong odour of scented shampoo by rolling around in the garden. Poop is especially good for getting rid of bath smells.

Hear your hooman shout in excitement. The more you roll, the more excited they'll get. Always please your hooman.

Some hoomans spend a lot of time and money to create flat pieces of grass called 'lawns'. These were made for you to dig in.

Flower beds were created for this purpose too.

Do not disappoint your hooman.

You can also roll around in them, especially if it's muddy.
see 'baths'

If you see your hooman with water leaking from their eyes, cuddle up to them and give them a big wet lick.

34

It will cheer them up tremendously!

A Doggie Handbook by Leia

Living with a hooman can be stressful...

But if you train them well, it can be one of the most rewarding things ever.

Handle every stressful
situation like we do.
Just pee on it and
walk away.

Live life like somebody
left the gate open.

Work Hard. Play Hard.
Fart Soft.

@the.official.dog.is

About myself

I started life in a puppy mill, where my friends and I were forced to produce the doggies that many people buy in pet shops. It was a hard life with no rest. Our babies were taken away from us after they were born. We lived in filthy cages that were too small for us. We were fed inferior food and dirty water. There were no doctors to treat us when we were sick.

We prayed very hard for a better life, and our prayers were answered. A man named Derrick showed up and rescued a group of us. We were all taken to a shelter, where I stayed for several months.

One sunny Saturday, I met a gentleman who came by to see some dogs. I was very excited and wagged my stump excitedly (my tail had been cut off in the mill). I soon found myself transported to a brand new home.

My first few months were spent visiting the vet. I had injuries from the mill that required lots of surgery. But with my adopted hooman standing shoulder to shoulder by my side, we weathered all storms.

Today, I help to keep the house in order.
I have spent many hours training my
hooman on all aspects of doggie life and
we have the most loving relationship.

xoxo

Leia 🐾

Buddy

Leia

Haru

Cory

Daisy

Toby

42

Adopting a Rescue

Sometimes, former breeding dogs like myself may seem a little shy, because we don't know what a home is.

All our lives, we have only known the inside of a cage. We don't know what a toilet is, nor a bedroom. In the puppy mill, it is the same place. I never saw a garden till I was rescued.

Bailey

Ciro

Zac

Chelsea

Mikoko

Toby

Gracie

Some of my fellow rescue dogs are afraid of collars and leashes. Others are afraid of loud noises. Big trucks and buses. Or large crowds.

Please be patient.

With your love, we will learn how to be dogs again!

44

Kaytee

Cole

Charcoal

About the illustrator

Black Mongrels is a creative agency founded by designer, art director and dog lover Hao Soh. He believes that when good holistic design serves to solve and not flaunt, true beauty blossoms and creativity thrives.

Just like the genetic make-up of a mongrel, whose ancestry flows from a diverse gene pool, the agency is a convergence of different expertise built upon the cornerstone of balance.

About the author

Daniel Boey is a creative director, fashion show producer, television personality and author who is affectionately known as the Godfather of Singapore Fashion. He is also fiercely passionate about rescue dogs and #AdoptNotShop.

He has appeared on three seasons of *Asia's Next Top Model* and written three books, including *We Adopted: A Collection of Dog Rescue Tales*.

He is proudest of being papa to Leia and godfather to a host of rescue dogs.

© 2020 Daniel Boey & Hao Soh

Published by Marshall Cavendish Editions
An imprint of Marshall Cavendish International

A member of the
Times Publishing Group

Other Marshall Cavendish Offices:
Marshall Cavendish Corporation, 99 White Plains Road, Tarrytown NY 10591-9001, USA •
Marshall Cavendish International (Thailand) Co Ltd, 253 Asoke, 12th Flr,
Sukhumvit 21 Road, Klongtoey Nua, Wattana, Bangkok 10110, Thailand •
Marshall Cavendish (Malaysia) Sdn Bhd, Times Subang, Lot 46, Subang Hi-Tech
Industrial Park, Batu Tiga, 40000 Shah Alam, Selangor Darul Ehsan, Malaysia.

Marshall Cavendish is a registered trademark of Times Publishing Limited

National Library Board, Singapore Cataloguing in Publication Data

Names: Boey, Daniel, 1965- | Soh, Hao, illustrator.
Title: How to train your hooman : a doggie handbook by Leia / assisted by her hooman, Daniel Boey ; with art and design by Hao @ Black Mongrels.
Description: Singapore : Marshall Cavendish Editions, [2020]
Identifiers: OCN 1126586933 | ISBN 978-981-4868-87-7 (hardback)
Subjects: LCSH: Dog adoption—Juvenile literature. | Rescue dogs—Juvenile literature. | Human-animal relationships—Juvenile literature.
Classification: DDC 636.0887—dc23

Printed in Singapore

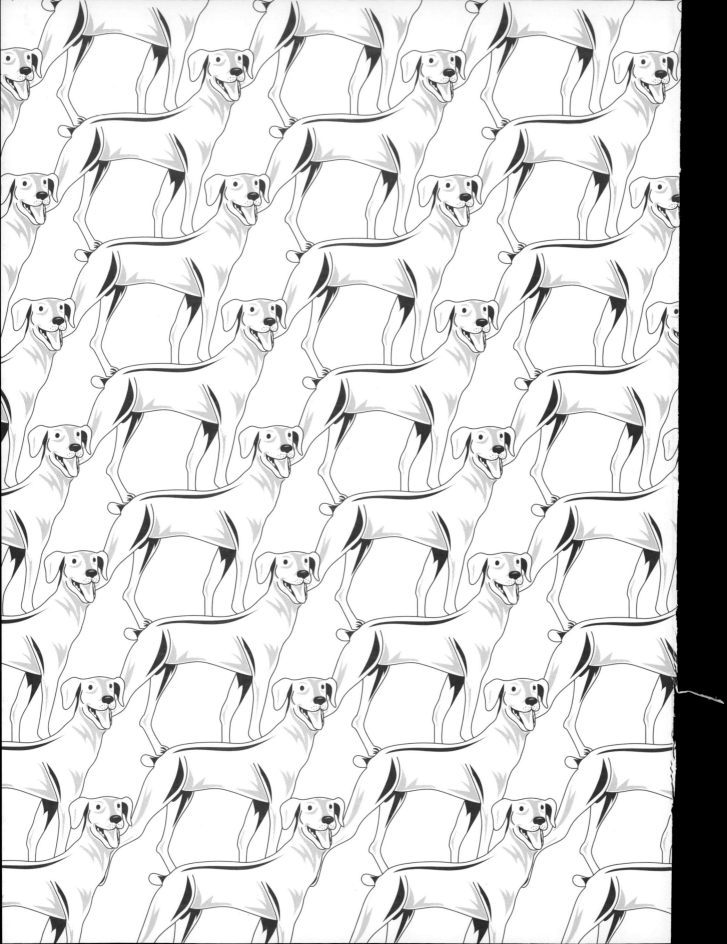